D0244160

Mr Bear's
NEW BABY

Debi Gliori

ORCHARD BOOKS

This book is dedicated
to families everywhere for whom
an uninterrupted night's sleep
is just a distant memory.

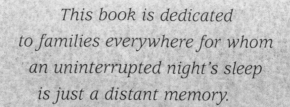

ORCHARD BOOKS
338 Euston Road, London NW1 3BH
Orchard Books Australia
Level 17/207 Kent Street, Sydney, NSW 2000
First published in 1999 by Orchard Books
This edition published in 2009 for Index Books Ltd.
ISBN: 978 1 84362 802 6
Text and illustrations © Debi Gliori
The right of Debi Gliori to be identified as the author and illustrator
of this work has been asserted by her in accordance with the Copyright,
Designs and Patents Act, 1988.
A CIP catalogue record for this book is available from the British Library.
Printed in China
1 3 5 7 9 10 8 6 4 2
Orchard Books is a division of Hachette Children's Books,
an Hachette UK company.
www.hachette.co.uk

It is way past bedtime in the forest.
It is time for everyone to be asleep.
A dark and quiet time for hush and lullabies.

But lights are on at Mr Bear's house.
And listen...drifting out over the trees
is the most awful din. It's the sound of
Mr Bear's new baby waking up.
"Oh dear," sighed Mrs Bear.
"Oh dear, oh dear," groaned Mr Bear.
"Waaaa," squeaked the new baby.

"What that baby needs is to be tucked in by her Daddy," said Mr Bear.

Mr Bear climbed out of bed and went to tuck in the new baby. He gazed lovingly at her.

But the baby squeaked more loudly.

"What that baby needs is some milk from her Mummy," said Mr Bear.

So Mrs Bear climbed out of bed and fed the new baby.

But the new baby spluttered and choked and squeaked some more.

Mr Bear paced up and down, patting the new baby's back. But the new baby closed her eyes, threw back her head and gave a huge squeak.

"Goodness," said Mr Bear, "what an enormous mouth for one so small. What you need is a lullaby."

Mr and Mrs Bear sang the new baby a lullaby. But that didn't work either.

Just then came a knock at the door.
In staggered Mr Rabbit-Bunn with a rocking cradle.

"Try this," he said, yawning. "When our babies were small, this used to put them to sleep."

So Mr Bear tucked his new baby in the cradle and they all took turns rocking her.

But the cradle was too wobbly, and still the new baby squeaked.

There was another knock on the door.
In came Mrs Hoot-Toowit with a huge nest.
  "I don't know if this will work," she said.
"But when Little Howl was a baby,
she always fell asleep in it at once."
  So Mr Bear put the new baby in the
nest. But the nest was too prickly and
the new baby continued to squeak.
  "Heavens," said Mr Bear, feeling
pretty close to squeaking himself,
"how can someone so small
make so much noise?"

One by one, all Mr Bear's sleepless neighbours
came calling with things to help the new baby sleep.

Mr Rivet-Frogge brought
his children's favourite lily-pad.
But that was too wet.

Mrs Buzz brought her infant's hive.
But that was too sticky.

Even Mrs Grizzle-Bear brought
Baby Grizzle-Bear's shawl.
But that was too woolly.

Mr Bear paced up and down.
"Little one," he said to the
sobbing baby. "My legs are tired
with all this walking."
The baby kept on crying.

"Baby bear," whispered Mr Bear. "My shoulder is soggy with all these tears." The baby cried all the more.

"Good grief," said Mr Bear, feeling tired, soggy and very fed up. "What on earth can I do to stop you crying?"

A little figure appeared at the door. "I can't sleep," said Small Bear. "That baby woke me up."

"You're too small to be up this late," groaned Mrs Bear. "Come on, back to bed."

"She's even smaller than I am," said Small Bear. "And *she's* up."

The new baby looked up with a woebegone little hiccup.

"I'm much bigger than both of you," sighed Mr Bear, "and all I want is *not* to be up."

"Is it that late?" said Mr Rabbit-Bunn and Mrs Hoot-Toowit.

"Bedtime," croaked Mr Rivet-Frogge.

"Sleep well," added Mrs Buzz.

"I'll come back for the shawl in the morning," said Mrs Grizzle-Bear.

The front door closed leaving
Mr and Mrs Bear with their
wakeful little bears.

"I know why the new baby is crying," said Small Bear. "It's because she wants someone to cuddle up to. Babies are like that," she said, burrowing deep into her father's arms.

"You're absolutely right, Small," said Mr Bear. "Let's see if a bedful of bears to cuddle into will help Baby Bear sleep, just this once."

Carrying their little bears,
Mr and Mrs Bear climbed
upstairs to bed.

Mr and Mrs Bear's bed wasn't wobbly or prickly.
Nor was it wet, sticky or woolly.
In fact it was utter bliss…
The new baby stopped crying immediately,
closed her eyes and fell fast asleep.

"My goodness," said Mr Bear, stunned by the sudden silence. "Well done, Small." But Small Bear was already fast asleep. "What a night," smiled Mrs Bear turning over and falling asleep.

The house was full of the sound of sleeping bears. All, that is, except for Mr Bear.

He lay in the dark and, far off in the trees, came the sound of Mrs Hoot-Toowit singing lullabies.

The baby stretched like a furry starfish.

"How can someone so small take up so much room?" thought Mr Bear.

The last thing he heard before he
fell asleep was Mrs Hoot-Toowit's,
"Goodnight, goodnight to you, to you."